Dear Parents,

The easy-to-read books in this series are based on The Puzzle Place™, public television's highly praised new show for children that teaches not ABC's or 123's, but "human being" lessons!

In these books, your child will learn about getting along with children from all different backgrounds, about dealing with problems, and making decisions—even when the best thing to do is not always so clear.

Filled with humor, the stories are about situations which all kids face. And best of all, kids can read them all on their own, building a sense of independence and pride.

So come along to the place where it all happens. Come along to The Puzzle Place™....

Copyright © 1996 by Lancit Copyright Corporation/KCET. All rights reserved. Published by Grosset & Dunlap, Inc.,
a member of The Putnam & Grosset Group, New York. GROSSET & DUNLAP is a trademark of Grosset & Dunlap,
Inc. THE PUZZLE PLACE and THE PUZZLE PLACE logo are trademarks of Lancit Media Productions, Ltd. and KCET.
Published simultaneously in Canada. Printed in the U.S.A. Library of Congress Catalog Card Number: 96-76135

ISBN 0-448-41313-2 A B C D E F G H I J

The Puzzle Place™ is a co-production of Lancit Media Productions, Ltd., and KCET/Los Angeles. Major funding
provided by the Corporation for Public Broadcasting and Edison International.

MY DOLL IS MISSING!

By Elizabeth Anders
Illustrated by Tom Brannon

Based on the teleplay,
"Beautiful Doll,"
by Ellis Weiner, Amy Hill,
and Judith Nihei.

GROSSET & DUNLAP · NEW YORK

Julie has a doll.

Her name is Suzie.

Suzie comes with her own
brush and comb.
She has hair that really grows.
Julie thinks that Suzie
is the best doll in the world.

One day, Julie takes Suzie
to The Puzzle Place.

"Oh, no! I forgot your brush!"
says Julie.
"Wait right here.
  I will go and get it."

But when Julie gets back,
Suzie is gone!
"Suzie!" calls Julie.
"Suzie, where are you?"

Nuzzle knows.

Nuzzle has taken Suzie.

Nuzzle wants to play with her.

Nuzzle does not know
that Julie is looking
for her doll.

Everybody is looking
for Suzie.
But no one is finding her.
"I know what we can do,"
Leon says.

"We can make pictures
of Suzie.
Then everyone will know
what she looks like."

So they make pictures.
They hang up the pictures
all around The Puzzle Place.

Inside...

...and outside.

The pictures say:

JULIE'S DOLL IS MISSING.

HAVE YOU SEEN HER?

Everybody wants to help.

They all want to do something.

And what does Julie do?

Julie starts to cry!
"Don't cry," says Kiki.
"We will find Suzie.
But until we do...
you can play with
my doll Yolanda."

"Thank you, Kiki,"
says Julie.
"Yolanda is very nice.
But she is just not Suzie."

"How about a bear?"
says Leon.
"No...you do not understand,"
says Julie.

"Suzie is special.

She is special because...

I love her.

Oh, where can Suzie be?"

Nuzzle knows.
He is having a lot of fun
with Suzie.
Until...

...Uh-oh.

Is this Julie's missing doll?

"You are in big trouble,"

says Sizzle.

"I am in big trouble,"
says Nuzzle.

"I will bring her back,"
says Nuzzle.
"You can't bring her back
like <u>that</u>," says Sizzle.

They try to fix Suzie up.

A little pat here.

A little lick there.

All done.

Now Nuzzle takes Suzie
back to Julie.
He does not want Julie
to be sad.

"Suzie! It's you!"
cries Julie.
"Nuzzle, did you have her
all the time?"

"Woof!" says Nuzzle.
He is showing Julie
that he is sorry.
And Julie understands.
She is just happy that...

...Suzie is back!